The Goodnight Train

JuNe SobeL

Illustrated by LauRa HuLiskA-BeitH

Houghton Mifflin Harcourt

Boston   New York

For information about permission to reproduce selections from
this book, write to trade.permissions@hmhco.com or to
Permissions, Houghton Mifflin Harcourt Publishing Company,
3 Park Avenue, 19th Floor, New York, New York 10016.

www.hmhco.com

The illustrations in this book were done in acrylic
paints with fabric and paper collage.
The display lettering was created by
Laura Huliska-Beith.
The text type was set in Pink Martini.

The Library of Congress has cataloged the
hardcover edition as follows:
The Goodnight Train/by June Sobel:
illustrated by Laura Huliska-Beith.
p. cm.
Summary: A child's bedtime ritual follows the
imaginary journey of a goodnight train's trip to
the Dreamland station.
[1. Bedtime—Fiction. 2. Railroads—Trains—Fiction.
3. Stories in rhyme.] I. Title: Goodnight Train.
II. Huliska-Beith, Laura, ill. III. Title.
PZ8.3.S692Go   2006
[E]—dc22   2004025169

ISBN: 978-0-15-205436-6 hardcover
ISBN: 978-1-328-74002-1 paperback
ISBN: 978-0-547-71898-9 board book
ISBN: 978-1-328-76438-6 lap board book

Manufactured in China
SGP 10 9 8 7 6 5 4
4500796654

To the memory of Clara Sobel,
who loved the world of books.
—J.S.

For Amelie, the newlywed, and Betty,
the newly graduated. Here's to new love,
new adventures, and more naps.
—L.H.B.

The Goodnight Train gets set to roll.
It's being shined and filled with coal.

Wash the cars off with a hose.
Scrub the engine's dirty nose.

Scrub-a-dub! Scrub-a-dub! Toot! Toot!

All aboard! The sun is down.
The Goodnight Train is leaving town.

Find your sleepers! Grab your teddy.
Climb right up! Your bed is ready!

Wheels are turning. Smoke drifts high,
painting clouds up in the sky.

Huff-a-puff-a! Huff-a-puff-a! ChoOOOOooo!
ChoOOOOooo!

Slumber, lumber up the hill.
Cars climb slowly up until...

Roll the corner, rock the curve.
Blankets bounce with every swerve.

Rock-a, rock-a, rock-a, rock-a—
Shhhhhhhhhh!
Shhhhhhhhhh!

Fly through a tunnel black as ink—
in and out before you blink.

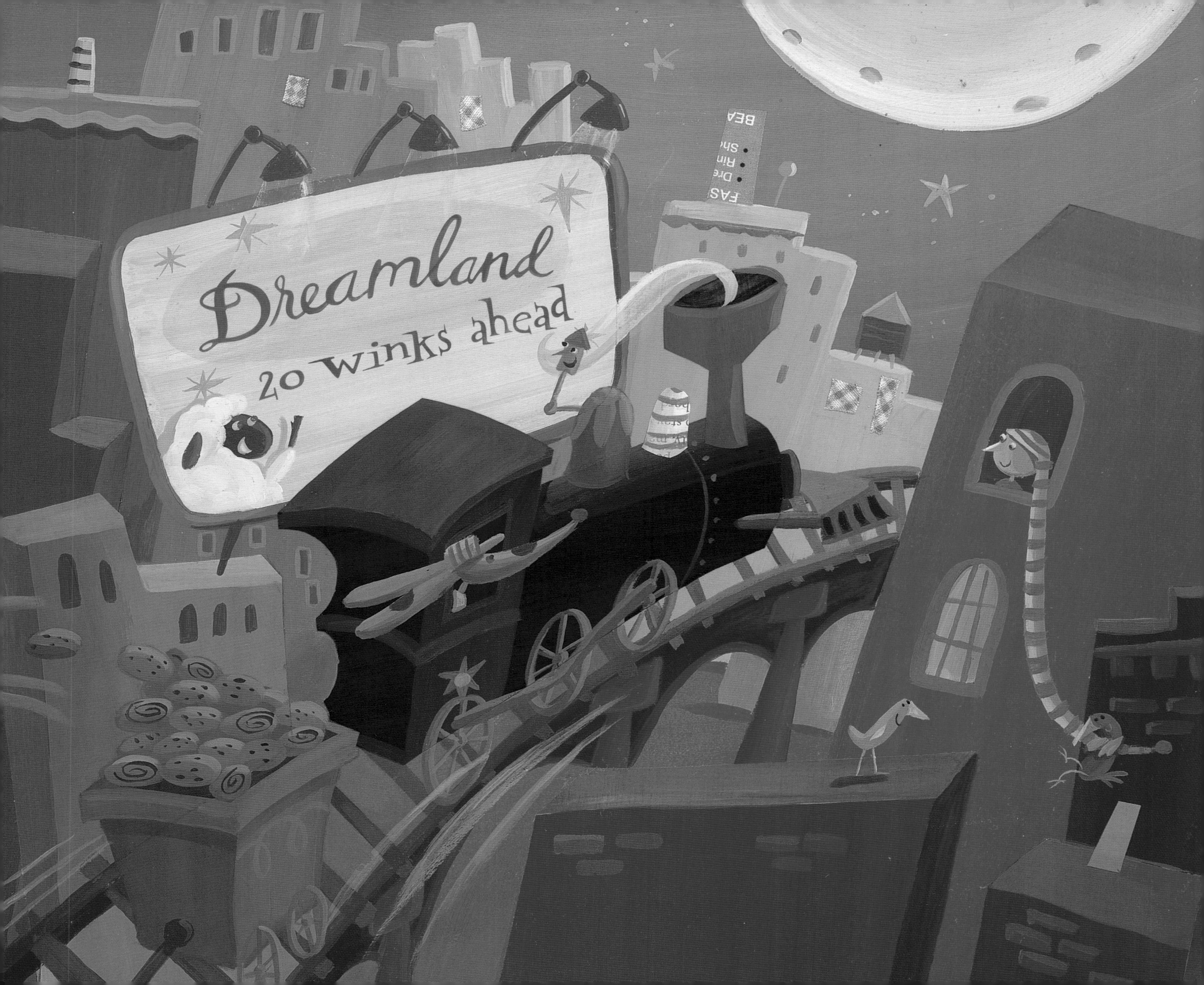
Dreamland
20 winks ahead

Catch that freight train whizzing past!
The Goodnight Train is moving fast!

Cars sway on the wooden track.
Wheels go click. Wheels go clack.

Glide across a plain so flat.
Gently toss this way and that.

CLICKETY - CLACK!
CLICKETY - CLACK!
CLICKETY - CLACK!

Curl through farms of fuzzy sheep.
The sleepy train slows to a creep.

Pushing toward the station's light,
cars crawl on with all their might.

Chug...chug...Chug!

"Sweet dreams ahead," the porter sighs.
The tired train can close its eyes.

Home at last, tucked in and snug,
the engine snores a final "Chug!"

Hush-a, hush-a, hush-a, hush-a— *Sleeeeeeeeep!*

Good night, train.
Good night.